The Lizards' Tale

By Mariama Ross

The Lizards' Tale

By Mariama Ross

Copyright © 2021 Mariama Ross

All rights reserved. No part of this publication may be reproduced, stored in any retrieval system, or transmitted in any form without the express consent of the author. The only exception is by a reviewer, who may quote short excerpts in a review.

ISBN: 978-0-578-88807-1

Visit the author's website at www.amaross.online

Dedication

I dedicate this book to all children who are curious about Africa.

This is Auntie Mariama's fie (house) in West Africa. This is Auntie Mariama.

She lived in a lovely little house on a hill overlooking the ocean.

One hot, sunny day, the Oppong lizard family was slowly moving down the road from Auntie Mariama's fie.

Soon they met another lizard family who cheerfully greeted them.

"**Ma aha** (Good Morning), fellow lizards," called Mr. Asare. "Where are you going this fine day?"

Oh, but why?" asked Mrs. Asare. "We heard it was a fine place to live.

We are rushing to move in there ourselves."

"Greetings," Mr. Oppong said glumly. "We are off to find a new home. Our old one has become unlivable."

"It used to be perfect," said Mrs. Oppong sadly, "But not anymore!" when that woman, Auntie Mariama, moved in, everything changed."

Mr. Oppong said, "We lived there for a whole year while the house was vacant and unspoiled by humans. It was our palace. But now..."

He shook his head sadly.

"Don't worry, dear," said
Mrs. Oppong in a soothing voice.
We will find another good home . . . somewhere."

Sister Asare piped up and asked,
"But why did you have to leave?"

"Well, for one thing, we lost many friends and relatives," said Mr. Oppong, "to The Shoe."

"The What???," shouted the Asares.

"The Shoe," Brother Oppong answered. "That woman chases lizards and smacks them with her flip-flop!"

"And The Broom," said Sister Oppong.

"She is really good at sweeping lizards off the walls with her broom!"

"Yeah," added Brother Oppong. "And she was always cleaning the place and spraying awful stuff to get rid of the insects that were our food.

YUCK!"

"Remember Uncle Mensah?" asked Mrs. Oppong.

"She chased him with her broom and he fell into a big spider web and got stuck! I shudder to think what happened to him!"

I know what happened to him," chipped in Sister Oppong.

"The Cat Monsters got him!

"Oh no, don't mention the Cat Monsters!" cried the Oppongs.

"Cat Monsters?" little Brother Asare asked in a shaky voice.

"What are Cat Monsters?"

Mr. Oppong explained slowly and painfully,
"Auntie Mariama has two cats who are very good hunters,
and their favorite food is . . ."

"Ok, ok, ok!" interrupted the Asares. Mrs. Asare shivered
and said, "We get the picture! Please say no more!"

"So that's why we left." said Mr. Oppong.
"We can't take the stress anymore. We're going to
find another vacant house where we can live
in peace again, at least until humans move in!"

Mr. Asare said, "That sounds like a wise plan. Mind if we join you?

"The more, the merrier. Bra! (Come!) Mr. Oppong shouted. "Just keep an eye out for Cat Monsters!"

So off they all went together in search of a brand new fie.

Extras →

Twi	English
Fie	House
Bra	Come
Ma aha	Good Morning
Medaase	Thank you

Ghana is Known for:

Its many castle-dungeons where kidnapped Africans were kept before transport to the West to be enslaved

Being a major grower of cocoa

Its fishing industry

Ghana is Known for:

Kakum National Forest and Canopy Walkway

Ghana is known for:

Being the original producer of the famous Kente cloth

And really cute kids

Excellent drummers

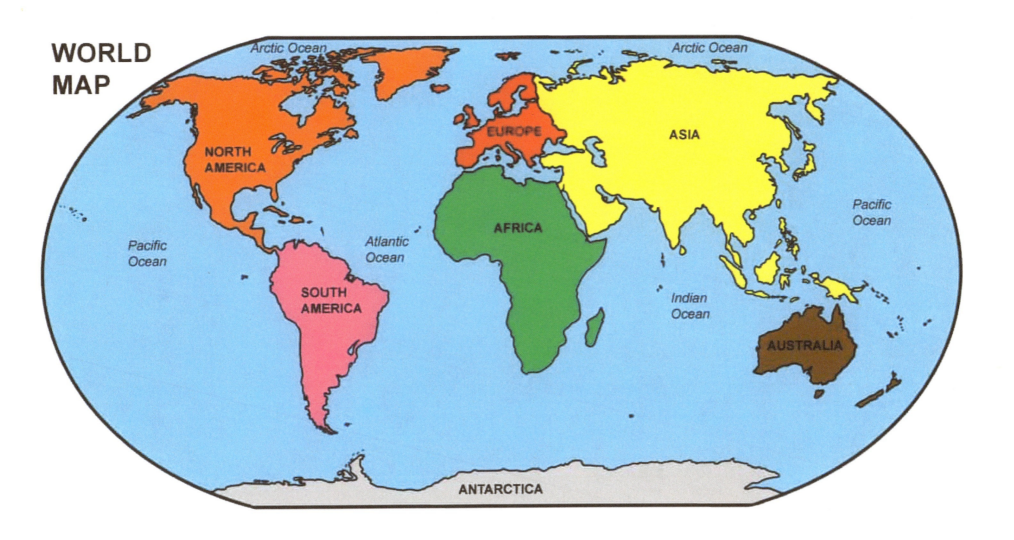

About the Author

Mariama Ross wrote and illustrated The Lizards' Tale. It is a whimsical tale, which, like all her stories, was inspired by real events from her many years living in Ghana and other African countries. An artist and career educator, she creates books to teach children about Africa, while sharing her love affair with this under-treated part or our world.

www.amaross.online

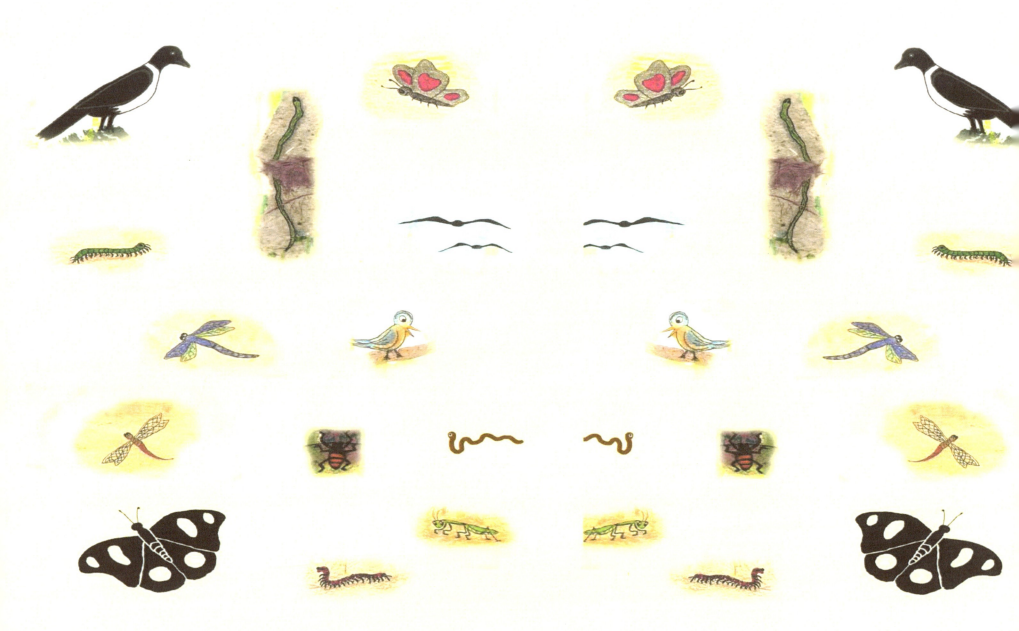

CPSIA information can be obtained
at www.ICGtesting.com
Printed in the USA
BVRC100852050521
606510BV00010B/91